Noah Bear

A day in the life of a young bear with autism

Written by: Dave Lawrence

Last night while my family were all fast asleep, I played and I bounced and I sang and I leaped.

I had so many things going on in my head; The last on the list was me sleeping in bed.

So hungry come morning, I screamed for my food.

I did not mean to be
so loud or rude.

It's just that I can't figure out the right words so they all come at once like a big flock of birds.

I find it so hard to be patient and share but I promise I'm really a good little bear.

The dirt and the rocks feel so good on my toes. Just wish I could get off these darn itchy clothes.

The second my mom and my dad look away. I race somewhere else to have fun and to play.

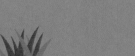

They both look so worried all the time on their face but in my defence, I thought it was a race.

I tried to explain it was all in good fun and just for the record, we all know that I won.

When we get home I am off in a flash, straight to the tub where I splish and I splash.

The bubbles they tingle and tickle my nose. This bear loves the water and makes sure it shows!

Somedays I just don't want to do any work. I'm trying to tell you but instead, go berserk.

I'm throwing this book because I can't just say that this isn't how I wanted to spend my day.

I don't roar at my family because I don't care so I script that I'm sorry to make the repairs.

I love my mom and my dad and my home.

I don't like how it feels when they mess with my hair

and if I'm being honest, it makes me quite scared.

These toys need some order, let's line them all up on every flat surface... even Henry our pup.

I wish I could tell you what I want to eat. I know it's not bedtime right now but I'm beat.

Brush all of my teeth first... I also don't like this. I'll say my good nights with a hug and a kiss.

Maybe tonight we will all get some rest or maybe my toys and I have a new quest.

This world sure is big and busy and loud and I know I don't do very well in a crowd.

But I'll try my best and just know I'm so glad that you both are so patient and my mom and dad.

The End